The Day Before Christmas

For Dana and Anna,
who love *The Nutcracker* too—E.B.

To Ben and Allie—B.P.

Clarion Books
a Houghton Mifflin Company imprint
215 Park Avenue South, New York, NY 10003
Text copyright © 1992 by Eve Bunting
Illustrations copyright © 1992 by Beth Peck
Printed in the U.S.A.

Library of Congress Cataloging-in-Publication Data
Bunting, Eve. 1928–
The day before Christmas / by Eve Bunting ; illustrated by Beth Peck.
p.   cm.
Summary: Four years after the death of her mother,
seven-year-old Allie goes with her grandfather to a
performance of "The Nutcracker" on Christmas Eve,
hears about the special day he had with her mother going to
her first "Nutcracker," and shares his loving memory of her.
ISBN 0-89919-866-X PA ISBN 0-618-05150-3
[1. Christmas—Fiction. 2. Ballet—Fiction. 3. Grandfathers—Fiction.
4. Mothers and daughters—Fiction.] I. Peck, Beth, ill. II. Title.
PZ7.B91527Dar 1992
[E]—dc20
                                                                91-35099
                                                                    CIP
                                                                     AC

BVG 10 9 8 7 6 5

The Day Before Christmas

EVE BUNTING

Paintings by Beth Peck

CLARION BOOKS · NEW YORK

It's the day before Christmas, and Grandpa and I are going to *The Nutcracker*. We are both dressed in our best clothes.

Dad and Jill drive us to the train station.

Jill is my stepmom. My own mom died when I was three so I hardly remember her. I like Jill a lot.

"Are you sure you and Jill don't want to come with us?" I ask Dad.
"No, Allie," he says. "This day is Grandpa's special gift to you. It should be just the two of you."

Jill kisses me. "But thanks for asking, honey. Have fun."

Then Dad takes me to one side. "Don't forget, Grandpa may be a little sad today. He'll be remembering."

I nod. But I'm hoping Grandpa isn't too sad. This is our special day.

"All aboard," the trainman calls, and Grandpa and I climb on.
He lets me sit by the window so I can see.
"Goodbye," we say as we wave. "Goodbye," and we're off,
going slowly at first, then faster and faster.

We glide past the backs of houses with winter-dry grass and for a while a dog runs beside the train, laughing up at us.

"Merry Christmas, Dog," I say.

Now there are fields with cows in them and we get a blue blink of ocean. Someone's surfing, even though it's winter, even though tomorrow's Christmas.

"Only in California," Grandpa says.

He has brought sandwiches and fruit in his little brown case. We pull down the folding tables and spread our picnic.

"Did you have a picnic like this last time?" I ask, and I think, Oh no! Asking will probably make him sad.

But Grandpa just says, "Yes. We had a picnic like this." And he doesn't look sad at all.

We roar importantly along while cars wait for us behind barricades, and then the train whistles high and loud.

"It smells the city," Grandpa says.

I sit on the edge of my seat. We're almost there.

The city station is grander than ours, with
wall paintings that go all the way to the ceiling
and a Christmas tree taller than I've ever seen.

A bus sits at the stop outside, as if waiting
for Grandpa and me. It wheezes us along
crowded streets under arches of silver bells.
I am so excited I can hardly breathe.

"Theatre Center," the driver calls, and he stops so Grandpa and I can get off.

And there it is, the theater, big and square with a banner across the front that says: THE NUTCRACKER. It's like a giant Christmas package waiting to be opened.

"I've never been to the theater before," I whisper.

"I know." Grandpa smiles. "Seven is a good age for your first *Nutcracker*."

A lady wearing white gloves shows us to our seats and the orchestra starts to play. Grandpa points out things to me on the program. We don't talk.

And then the music plays more loudly, the rustlings stop, the curtain goes up.

It's *Nutcracker* time.

And oh, it's wonderful! There's a Sugar Plum Fairy and an army of giant mice and the handsome Nutcracker himself on his wooden horse. We're magicked away to a land of puppets and dolls and candy people and I don't want it ever to end.

"Bravo!" we call. "Bravo!"
The dancers have to come back three times to bow
and throw kisses to the audience. It's hard to let them go.

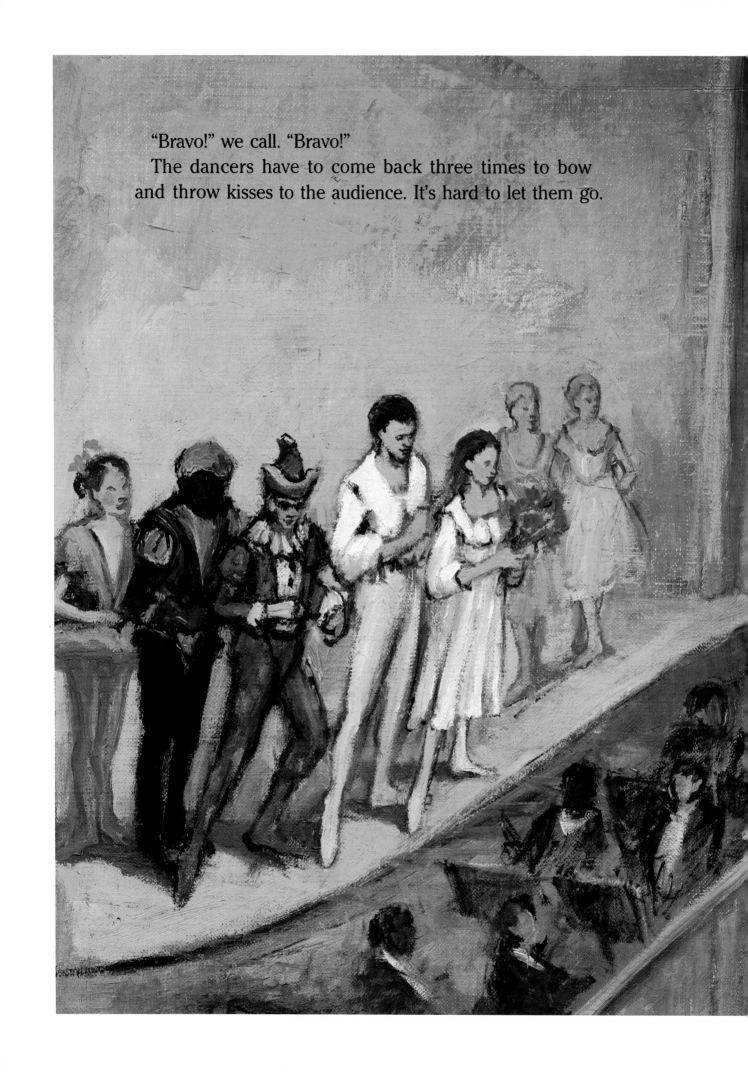

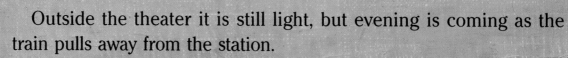

Outside the theater it is still light, but evening is coming as the train pulls away from the station.

I sigh. "Our special day is nearly over."

Grandpa touches my hair. "A special day is never over."

We divvy up the raisins left from lunch and then sit back against the soft train cushions.

"Grandpa?" I ask. "Can you tell me about the special day you had with Mom?"

Grandpa closes his eyes. "It was Christmas Eve, all those years ago. Your mom was seven, same as you. She loved *The Nutcracker*, too."

"What was her favorite part?"

"The snow fairies."

I close my eyes, too, and let the snow fairies spin and twirl like ice flakes in my mind. It's nice to be doing what my mom did when she was my age. It brings her close, as if she and Grandpa and I are all here together.

"She always remembered her first *Nutcracker*," Grandpa says.

"I'll remember mine, too."

I push my hand into his. "Dad was afraid you might be sad today."

Grandpa smiles his nicest smile. "I'm not. A loving memory is happy, not sad. Isn't it good that you and I are starting some new memories, Allie?"

"Really good," I say. "Merry Christmas, Grandpa."

"Merry Christmas, Allie."

I close my eyes and let the snow fairies spin and twirl like ice flakes in my mind. It's nice to be doing what my mom did when she was my age. It brings her close, as if she and Grandpa and I are all here together.

"She always remembered her first *Nutcracker*," Grandpa says.

"I'll remember mine, too."

"Seven-year-old Allie goes on a special outing, by train, with her grandfather to see *The Nutcracker*—her first trip to the theater. It's also a poignant commemoration: Grandpa took Allie's mother, who died when Allie was three, to a Christmas Eve performance of the ballet the year *she* was seven. Responding to Allie's anxious sympathy, Grandpa explains that he's not sad: 'A loving memory is happy.' . . . Peck's freely painted oils . . . leave the canvas exposed, effectively portraying a California setting some time ago. . . . An evocative vignette."

—*Kirkus Reviews*

$5.95

ISBN 0-618-05150-3

90000

9 780618 051502

1-11001
0900

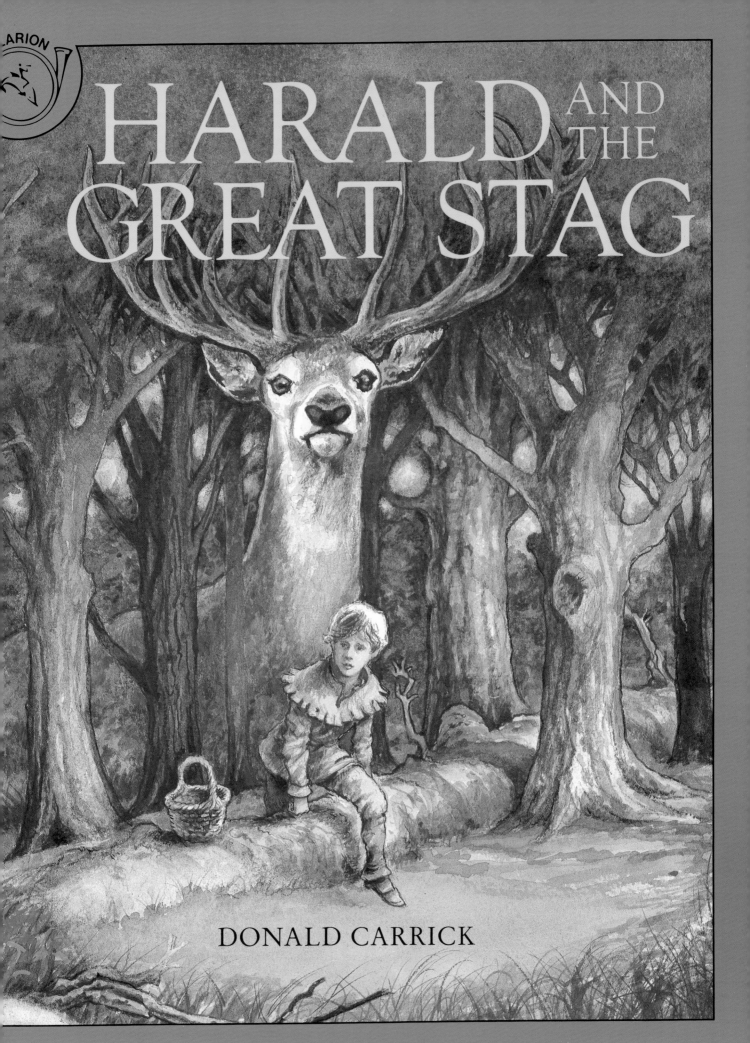

HARALD AND THE GREAT STAG

DONALD CARRICK